Faber
Stories

Celia Fremlin (1914–2009) was born in Kent. Her first published novel of suspense was *The Hours Before Dawn* (1958), which went on to win the Mystery Writers of America's Edgar Award for Best Novel in 1960. Over the next thirty-five years Fremlin published a further eighteen titles.

Celia
Fremlin

Ghostly
Stories

Faber
Stories

ff

First published in this edition in 2019
by Faber & Faber Limited
Bloomsbury House
74–77 Great Russell Street
London WC1B 3DA

Typeset by Faber & Faber Limited
Printed and bound by CPI Group (UK) Ltd, Croydon, CR0 4YY

A CIP record for this book
is available from the British Library

ISBN 978–0–571–35684–3

10 9 8 7 6 5 4 3 2 1

The Hated House

Now that she had it to herself, Lorna felt that she could almost enjoy hating her home so much. She flung her school coat and beret on to the sofa, dumped her satchel down in the middle of the floor, and watched with satisfaction as the books and papers spilled out over her mother's spotless, well-vacuumed carpet. It was nice to be able to mess it up like that, without risk of reprimand. She gazed round the neat, firelit room with contempt. Hideous ornaments—houseplants, bric-à-brac of all kinds; and on either side of the fire those two neat, well upholstered armchairs were drawn up, for all the world as if a happily married couple habitually sat in them; a contented couple, smiling at each other across the hearth; not a couple like Lorna's parents, wrangling, bickering, squabbling, the long evenings filled with temper or with tears . . .

With slatternly, spread-eagled violence, Lorna flung herself into the nearest of the two chairs, sending it skidding and scratching under her weight across the polished wood surround.

That was better! Lorna spread out the length of her legs untidily, in the luxurious abandonment of solitude: real, reliable, long-term solitude, a whole glorious evening of it, and a whole night to follow!

Such a fuss there had been, about this simple business of leaving her alone in the house for a night! Just as if she had been a baby, instead of a young woman of nearly sixteen!

"Be sure you bolt all the doors," her mother had said, not once but fifty times: "Be sure you put the guard in front of the fire before you go to bed . . . Be sure you turn off the oven . . . Be sure you don't answer the door to anyone you don't know . . . Remember you can always go in to the Holdens if you feel in the least bit nervous . . ."

Go in to the Holdens, indeed! Lorna would have died—yes, she would willingly have lain right here on the carpet with her throat cut—before she would run for help to that dreary Holden woman, both boring and sly, chatter chatter over the wall to

Mummy about the problems of teenage daughters. Ugh!

Ah, but this was the life! Lorna slid yet deeper and more luxuriously into the cushioned depths of the chair. Tea when she liked; supper when she liked; homework when she liked; music when she liked. Lorna's eyes turned with lazy anticipation towards the pile of pop records stacked under the record player. Ah, the fuss there usually was over those records, with Mummy twittering in and out, trying to stop Daddy being annoyed by them . . . "Can't you turn it down lower, dear? . . . Can't you play them in the afternoons when Daddy's not here? You know how it annoys him."

What Mummy didn't realize was that actually it was quite fun annoying Daddy—a real roaring bellowing row instead of all these anxious twitterings! And afterwards Daddy would go on yelling at Mummy for hours, long after the records were finished and done with. And then next day Mummy would scuttle about with red eyes, polishing things, as if a tidy polished house was some sort of protection against quarrelling! Honestly, *adults*! That's why I hate the smell of polish, thought Lorna, deliberately jolting the chair on its rusty castors back and forth across the polished boards, making deep dents and scratches in the wood. It's misery-polish that Mummy puts on everything, it's dishonesty-polish, trying to make this look like a happy home when it isn't! It's because she's too cowardly, too much of a doormat, to stand up to Daddy's tempers, so she tidies the house instead . . . I bet she's tidied the kitchen even better than usual today, just because she's nervous about leaving me alone! She thinks tidiness is a substitute for everything! Stirred by a flicker of resentful curiosity, and also by a mounting interest in the thought of tea, Lorna dragged herself from her luxurious position, and went to the kitchen to investigate.

Yes, it was immaculate. Every surface scrubbed and shining; a delicious little dish of cold chicken and salad all ready for Lorna's supper; and for her tea—just look! a big, expensive, once-in-a-lifetime meringue, bursting with cream! A *treat*! Another of

Mummy's pathetic attempts to provide Lorna with at least the shell of a happy home! Irritation fought in Lorna with eager appetite. Does she think I'm a baby, or something, who needs to be consoled for its Mummy being away? I *love* Mummy being away! I love it! I love it!—and with each "love" her teeth sank deeper into the rare, luscious thing; the cream spurted with bounteous prodigality across her cheeks, and she didn't even have to wipe them, because she was alone. Alone, alone, alone: the nearest thing to Paradise.

Outside, the spring evening was fading. The sob and thrum of Lorna's favourite records mingled first with a pink sunset light in the pale room; then with a pearly, silvery greyness against which the firelight glowed ever more orange and alive; and at last, curtains drawn, lamps switched on, coal piled recklessly into a roaring blaze, it was night; and still the records played on, over and over again. It was too lovely a time, this time of firelight and perfect solitude, to waste on anything less beautiful than the music which her parents hated so.

It was nearly nine o'clock when the telephone began to ring. It began just as Lorna had settled herself cosily by the fire with her tray of chicken salad, new rolls, and a huge mug of boiling hot, sweet black coffee, whose deliciousness was enhanced by the fact that Mummy would have said: Don't have it black, dear, not at this time of night, it'll keep you awake.

Damn! she thought, setting down the mug just in the middle of the first glorious sip. Damn! and then: Why don't I just not answer it? Why don't I ignore it? I bet it'll just be Mummy, fussing about something. Yes, driving along those monotonous miles of motorway, she'll have been thinking up some new things to fuss about: Have I latched the kitchen window? Have I brought the milk in off the step? Will I be sure and shut the spare room window if it rains? Fuss, fuss, fuss, an expensive long-distance fuss from a roadside callbox . . . I *won't* answer, why should I? I'll just let it ring, serve her right, teach her a lesson, show her I'm not a baby . . . Defiantly, Lorna raised the mug to her lips once more, and calmly, leisurely, she resumed her sipping.

But how the telephone kept on! It was irritating, it was spoiling this solitary, delightful meal which she had planned to savour to the full. She laid down her knife and fork restlessly. Weren't they *ever* going to ring off? How long *do* people go on ringing before they finally give up? . . . and just then, at last, with a despairing little hiccup, the telephone ceased ringing.

Silence swung back into the room, and flooded Lorna with relief. She picked up her knife and fork once more, and prepared to recapture her interrupted bliss. Having a meal alone by the fire like this. *Alone!* The joy of it! No table-manners. No conversation. Just peace, delicious peace.

But somehow it had all been spoiled. The slow, savoury mouthfuls tasted of almost nothing now; the new, favourite magazine propped against the coffee-pot could not hold her attention; and she was conscious of an odd tenseness, a waiting, listening unease in every nerve. She finished the meal without enjoyment, and as she carried the tray out to the kitchen the telephone began again.

The shock was somehow extraordinary. Almost dropping the tray on to the kitchen table, Lorna turned and ran headlong back into the sitting-room slamming the door behind her as if that would somehow protect her from the imperious, nagging summons. All her sense of guilt and unease at not having answered before seemed to make it doubly impossible to answer now; and the longer she let it ring, the more impossible it became. Why should anybody ring so long, and so persistently? If it was Mummy, then surely she would have assumed by now that Lorna had gone in to the Holdens? Who else could it be who would ring, and ring, and ring like this? Surely no one goes on ringing a number *for ever*? Oh, please God, make it stop!

And at last, of course, it did stop; and again the silence filled her ears in a great flood, but this time there was no relief in it. She felt herself so tense, so tightly listening, it was almost as if she knew, deep in her knotted stomach, just what was going to happen next.

It was a light, a very light footstep on the garden path that next caught at her hearing; lightly up the steps, and then a fumbling at the front door. Not a knock; not a ring; just a fumbling, as of someone trying to unlock the door; someone too weak, or too blind, to turn the key.

"Be sure you bolt all the doors . . ." In her head Lorna seemed to hear these boring, familiar instructions not for the fiftieth time, but for the first . . . "Be sure you latch the kitchen window . . . Don't answer the door to anyone you don't know . . ."

Lorna tiptoed out into the hall, and for a few moments she fancied that she must have imagined the sounds, for all was quiet. No shadowy silhouette could be seen looming against the frosted panels of the door, palely glittering in the light of the street lamp. But even as she stood there, the flap of the letter-box began to stir, slowly. Lorna was looking into an eye.

A single eye, of course, as it would be if anyone is peering through a letter-box; and yet, irrationally, it was this singleness that shocked most, carrying one back, in an instant, beyond the civilized centuries, right back to the Cyclops, to the mad, mythical beginnings of mankind. Lorna began to scream.

"Don't be frightened," came a voice from outside—a young voice, Lorna registered with gasping thankfulness and surprise. Why, it was a *girl's* voice: a girl no older than herself by the sound of it! "Don't be frightened, Lorna—but do please let me in!"

Reassured completely by the sound of her own name, Lorna ran to the door and flung it open.

"Oh, you *did* give me a fright—" she was beginning, but then stopped, puzzled. For though the girl standing there looked vaguely familiar, and was roughly her own age, Lorna did not know her. She had taken for granted, when she heard herself addressed by name, that she would be bound to recognize the speaker.

"Hallo! I—that is, I'm awfully sorry, I'm sure I ought to know you—?" she began uncertainly.

"It's all right; I didn't think you would recognize me at once," answered the girl, stepping confidently into the hall, and looking round her. "I hope you don't mind my coming out of the blue like this; but I used to live here, you see."

She was a forceful looking girl, Lorna could see now, standing there under the hall light; with strong black hair springing from a high, very white forehead, and her eyes were dark, and snapping bright; as if, thought Lorna, she had a quick temper and a quick wit, and very much a will of her own.

"Oh, I see." Lorna tried to collect her wits. This must be the daughter of the family who had lived here before Lorna's family had moved in, seven or eight years ago. "Oh, I see—Fancy you remembering my name! Do come in—I expect you'd like to look at everything, see how it's changed since you were here." Already she felt that she was going to like this girl, who was looking round with such bright interest, and seemed so friendly. "I'll show you my room first, shall I; I wonder if it was the same one you had? It's the little back one that looks out on the garden."

By the time they had explored the house, Lorna felt as if she and this other girl had known each other for years. They seemed to have so much the same tastes, the same loves and hates; and as they sat over the fire afterwards, with a newly made pot of coffee between them, Lorna found herself confiding in her new friend all her troubles: Daddy's tempers; Mummy's doormat submission to him, her anxious, fussy housekeeping.

"I wouldn't mind," she explained, "if Mummy was *really* a houseproud sort of person—if she really got any pleasure out of making the house look nice. But she doesn't. She does it in a desperate sort of way. She clutters everything up with flowers, and hideous ornaments—"

"—as if it was a substitute for making you and your father happy, you mean?" put in the other girl quickly. "You mean, since she can't give you a happy home, she's determined to give you a neat, clean one, full of things?"

"That's it! That's it exactly!" cried Lorna. "How well you understand! But why such *ugly* things?" Her eyes swept the mantelpiece and the crowded corner cupboard. "It's as if she collected ugly things on purpose."

"I don't think so," said the other girl quickly, glancing rapidly round the room. "They're not actually ugly, you know—not each of them taken singly. It's just that nobody loves them—your mother and father never chose any of them together, in a little dark shop, on holiday when they were enjoying themselves. I expect your mother bought them pretending it was like that when it wasn't."

"Why, yes! I expect she did! That would be exactly like her!" cried Lorna, enchanted. Never had she found anyone before who could understand the way this girl understood. "That's why I hate them so—"

"So let's smash them," said the other girl, in the same quiet, thoughtful tones. "Let's bash them to pieces on the marble fireplace there. Think how they'd crash and shatter!" There was a strange gleam in her dark eyes, and Lorna stared at her, for the first time uneasy. But she was joking—of course she was.

"Wouldn't I just love to!" Lorna gave a little laugh appropriate to such nonsense. "Have some more coffee?"

"No. I mean it. Let's! You hate them—you are right to hate them. Hateful things should be s-s-s-s-mashed!" And snatching a china shepherdess from the mantelpiece, the girl flung it with all her force into the grate.

The splintering, shocking, unimaginable crash shocked Lorna speechless. "Stop!" she tried to cry as a teapot and two vases burst like spray across the hearthrug; and then, even as she gasped out her protests, something extraordinary began to seep into her soul. Shock, yes; but what was this joy, this exultation, this long pent-up anger, as crash followed crash and splinters of china rebounded across the room like hail?

"Smash them! Smash them!" the girl was crying, her dark face alight with extraordinary joy. "Rip up the cushions! Tear down the curtains—they were sewn in misery, not in love, every stitch was stitched in misery!" With a great rending, ripping sigh, the curtains huddled to the floor; and by now both girls were upon them, ripping, tearing. A madness not her own was in Lorna now, and she too was tearing, smashing, hurling, in an ecstasy of shared destruction such as she had never dreamed.

Dreamed? *Was* she dreaming, then? Was this the telephone waking her, ringing, ringing, ringing across the devastated room? This time, Lorna ran instantly to answer, snatched it from its hook and waited.

Yes. Yes, this was the home of Mrs Mary Webster. Yes, I'm her daughter. No, I'm afraid my father is not in. You rang several times before? Oh. Yes what is it? What is it?

An accident. My dear, I'm very, very sorry to have to tell you . . . an accident . . . your mother. Yes. Your mother . . . a lorry out of a side road . . . it must have been instantaneous . . . And a lot more, kindly, helpful, sympathetic, kind people on their way to Lorna right now. Lorna couldn't really take it in.

She was not surprised, when she went slowly back to the sitting-room, to find that her new friend was gone. She had known that she would be gone, for she knew, now, who it must have been. For who else was there who could have hated the room as Lorna hated it, and would have come back, at the last, to destroy it?

And, after all, the destruction was not so very great; for a ghost, even using all its strength, is not strong as a living person is strong. A few things were broken, the curtains crumpled and awry; and as Lorna sat down among the mussed cushions she was crying: crying with happiness because she and her mother—her real mother, the one hidden beneath the doormat exterior for all these years—had understood each other at the last.

The New House

Looking back, I find it hard to say just when it was that I first began to feel anxious about my niece, Linda. No—anxious is not quite the right word, for of course I have been anxious about her many times during the ten years she has been in my care. You see, she has never been a robust girl, and when she first came to live with me, a nervous, delicate child of twelve, she seemed so frail that I really wondered sometimes if she would survive to grow up. However, I am happy to say that she grew stronger as the years passed, and I flatter myself that by gentle, common-sense handling and abundant affection I have turned her into as strong and healthy a young woman as she could ever have hoped to be. Stronger, I am sure, (though perhaps I shouldn't say this) than she would have been if my poor sister had lived to bring her up.

No, it was not anxiety about Linda's health that had troubled me during the past weeks; nor was it simply a natural anxiety about the wisdom of her engagement to John Barlow. He seemed a pleasant enough young man, with his freckled, snub-nosed face and ginger hair. Though I have to admit I didn't really take to him myself—he made me uneasy in some way I can't describe. But I would not dream of allowing this queer prejudice of mine to stand in the way of the young couple—there is nothing I detest more than this sort of interference by the older generation.

All the same, I must face the fact that it was only after I heard of their engagement that I began to experience any qualms of fear about Linda—those first tremors of a fear that was to grow and grow until it became an icy terror that never left me, day or night.

I think it was in September that I first became aware of my uneasiness—a gusty September evening with autumn in the wind—in the trees—everywhere. I was cycling up the long gentle hill from the village after a particularly wearisome and inconclusive committee meeting of the Women's

Institute. I was tired—so tired that before I reached the turning into our lane I found myself getting off my bicycle to push it up the remainder of the slope —a thing I have never done before. For in spite of my fifty-four years I am a strong woman, and a busy one. I cycle everywhere, in all weathers, and it is rare indeed for me to feel tired, certainly the gentle incline between the village and our house had never troubled me before. But tonight, somehow, the bicycle might have been made of lead—I felt as if I had cycled fifteen miles instead of the bare one and a half from the village; and when I turned into the dripping lane, and the evening became almost night under the overhanging trees, I became aware not only of tiredness, but of an indefinable foreboding. The dampness and the autumn dusk seemed to have crept into my very soul, bringing their darkness with them.

Well, I am not a fanciful woman. I soon pulled myself together when I reached home, switched on the lights, and made myself a cup of tea. Strong and sweet it was, the way I always like it. Linda often laughs at me about my tea—she likes hers so thin and weak that I sometimes wonder why she bothers to pour the water into the teapot at all, instead of straight from the kettle to her cup!

So there I sat, the comfortable old kitchen chair drawn up to the glowing stove, and I waited for the warmth and the sweet tea to work their familiar magic. But somehow, this evening, they failed. Perhaps I was really *too* tired; or perhaps it was the annoyance of noticing from the kitchen clock that it was already after eight. As I have told you, I am a busy woman, and to find that tiresome meeting must have taken a good two hours longer than usual *was* provoking, especially as I had planned to spend a good long evening working on the Girls' Brigade accounts.

Whatever it may have been, somehow I couldn't relax. The stove crackled merrily; the tea was delicious; yet still I sat, tense and uneasy, as if waiting for something.

And then, somehow, I must have gone to sleep, quite suddenly; because the next thing I knew I was dreaming. Quite a simple, ordinary sort of dream it will seem to you—nothing alarming, nothing even unusual in it, and yet you will have to take my word for it that it had all the quality of a nightmare.

I dreamed that I was watching Linda at work in the new house. I should explain here that for the past few months Linda has not been living here with me, but in lodgings in the little town where she works, about six miles from here. It is easier for her getting to and from the office, and also it means that she and John can spend their evenings working at the new house they have been lucky enough to get in the Estate on the outskirts of the town. It is not quite finished yet, and they are doing all the decorations themselves—I believe John is putting up shelves and cupboards and all kinds of clever fittings. I am telling you this so that you will see that there was nothing intrinsically nightmarish about the setting of my dream—on the contrary, the little place must have been full of happiness and bustling activity—the most unlikely background for a nightmare that you could possibly imagine.

Well, in my dream I was there with them. Not with them in any active sense, you understand, but hovering in that disembodied way one does in dreams—an observer, not an actor in the scene. Somewhere near the top of the stairs I seemed to be, and looking down I could see Linda through the door of one of the empty little rooms. It was late afternoon in my dream, and the pale rainy light gleamed on her flaxen-pale hair making it look almost metallic—a sort of shining grey. She had her back to me, and she seemed absorbed in distempering the far wall of the room—I seemed to hear that suck-sucking noise of the distemper brush with extraordinary vividness.

And as I watched her, I began to feel afraid. She looked so tiny, and thin, and unprotected; her fair, childlike head seemed poised somehow so precariously on her white neck—even her absorption in the painting seemed in my dream to add somehow to her peril. I opened my mouth to warn her—of I know not what—but I could make no sound, as is the way of dreams. It was then that the whole thing slipped into nightmare. I tried to scream—to run—I struggled in vain to wake up—and as the nightmare mounted I became aware of footsteps, coming nearer and nearer through the empty house. "It's only John!" I told myself in the dream, but even as the words formed themselves in my brain, I knew I had touched the very core of my terror. This man whose every glance and movement had always filled me with uneasiness—already the light from some upstairs room was casting his shadow, huge and hideous, across the landing . . . I struggled like a thing demented to break the paralysis of nightmare. And then, somehow, I was running, running, running . . .

I woke up, sick and shaking, the sweat pouring down my face. For a moment I thought a great hammering on the door had woken me, but then I realized that it was only the beating of my heart, thundering and pounding so that it seemed to shake the room.

Well, I have told you before that I am a strong woman, not given to nerves and fancies. Linda is the one who suffers from that sort of thing, not me. Time and again in her childhood I had to go to her in the night and soothe her off to sleep again after some wild dream. But for *me*, a grown woman, who never in her life has feared or run away from anything—for *me* to wake up weak and shaking like a baby from a childish nightmare! I shook it off angrily, got out of my chair and fetched my papers, and, as far as I can remember, worked on the Girls' Brigade accounts far into the night.

I thought no more about it until, perhaps a week or so later, the same thing happened again. The same sort of rainy evening, the same coming home quite unusually tired—and then the same dream. Well, not quite the same. This time Linda wasn't distempering; she was on hands and knees—staining the floor or something of the sort. And there were no footsteps. This time nothing happened at all; only there was a sense of evil, of brooding hatred, which seemed to fill the little house. Somehow I felt it to be focussed on the little figure kneeling in its gaily patterned overall. The hatred seemed to thicken round her—I could feel giant waves of it converging on her, mounting silently, silkily till they hung poised above her head in ghastly, silent strength. Again I tried to scream a warning; again no sound came; and again I woke, weak and trembling, in my chair.

This time I was really worried. The tie between me and Linda is very close—closer, I think, than the tie between her and her mother could ever have been. Common-sense sort of person though I am, I could not help wondering whether these dreams were not some kind of warning. Should I ring her up, and ask if everything was all right? I scolded myself for the very idea! I mustn't give way to such foolish, hysterical fancies—I have always prided myself on letting Linda lead her own life, and not smothering her with possessive anxiety as her mother would have done. Stop! I mustn't keep speaking of Linda's mother like this—of Angela—of my own sister. Angela has been dead many years now, and whatever wrong I may have suffered from her once has all been forgotten and forgiven years ago—I am not a woman to harbour grievances. But, of course, all this business of Linda's approaching marriage was bound to bring it back to me in a way. I couldn't help remembering that I, too, was once preparing a little house ready for my marriage; that Richard once looked into my eyes just as John now looks into Linda's.

Well, I suppose most old maids have some ancient—and usually boring—love story hidden somewhere in their pasts, and I don't think mine will interest you much—it doesn't even interest me after all these years, so I will tell it as briefly as I can.

When I fell in love with Richard I was already twenty-eight, tall and angular, and a school-teacher into the bargain. So it seemed to me like a miracle that he, so handsome, gay and charming should love me in return and ask me to marry him. Our only difficulty was that my parents were both dead, and

I was the sole support of my young sister, Angela. We talked it over, and decided to wait a year, until Angela had left school and could support herself.

But at the end of the year it appeared that Angela had set her heart on a musical career. Tearfully she begged me to see her through her first two years at college; after that, she was sure she could fend for herself.

Well, Richard was difficult this time, and I suppose one can hardly blame him. He accused me of caring more for my sister than for him, of making myself a doormat, and much else that I forget. But at last it was agreed to wait for the two years, and meantime to work and save for a home together.

And work and save we did. By the end of the two years we had bought a little house, and we spent our evenings decorating and putting finishing touches to it, just as Linda and John are doing now.

Then came another blow. Angela failed in her exams. Again I was caught up in the old conflict; Richard angry and obstinate, Angela tearful and beseeching me to give her one more chance, for only six months this time. Once again I agreed, stipulating that this time was really to be the last. To my surprise, after his first outburst, Richard became quite reasonable about it; and soon after that he was sent away on a series of business trips, so that we saw much less of each other.

Then, one afternoon at the end of May, not long before the six months were up, something happened. I was sitting on the lawn correcting exercises when Angela came out of the house and walked slowly towards me. I remember noticing how sweetly pretty she looked with her flaxen hair and big blue eyes—just like Linda's now. The spring sunshine seemed to light up the delicacy of her too-pale skin, making it seem rare and lovely. She sat down on the grass beside me without speaking, and something in her silence made me lay down my pen.

"What is it, Angela?" I said. "Is anything the matter?"

She looked up at me then, her blue eyes full of childish defiance, and a sort of pride.

"Yes," she said. "I'm going to have a baby." She

paused, looking me full in the face. "Richard's baby."

I didn't say anything. I don't even remember feeling anything. Even then, I suppose, I was a strong-minded person who did not allow her feelings to run away with her. Angela was still talking:

"And it's no use blaming *us*, Madge." She was saying. "What do you expect, after you've kept him dangling all these years?"

I remember the exercise book open in front of me, dazzling white in the May sunshine. One of the children had written "Nappoleon"—like that, with two p's—over and over again in her essay. There must have been half a dozen of them just on the one page. I felt I would go mad if I had to go on looking at them, so I took my pen and crossed them out, one after another, in red ink. Even to this day I have a foolish feeling that I would still go mad if I ever saw "Nappoleon" spelt like that again.

I felt as if a long time had passed, and Angela must have got up and gone away ages ago; but no, here she was, still talking:

"Well, *you* may not care, Madge," she was saying; "I don't suppose you'd stop correcting your old exercises if the world blew up. But what about *me*? What am I to *do*?"

I simply had to cross out the last of the "Nappoleon's" before I spoke.

"Do?" I said gently, "Why, Richard must marry you, of course. I'll talk to him myself."

Well, they were married, and Linda was born, a delicate, sickly little thing, weighing barely five pounds. Angela, too, was poorly. She had been terribly nervous and ill during her pregnancy and took a long time to recover; and it was tacitly agreed that there should be no more children. A pity, because I know Richard would have liked a large family. Strange how I, a strong healthy woman who could have raised half a dozen children without turning a hair, should have been denied the chance, while poor, sickly Angela . . . Ah well, that is life. And I suppose my maternal feelings were largely satisfied by caring for poor delicate little Linda—it seemed only natural that when first her father and then

Angela died the little orphan should come and live with me. And indeed I loved her dearly. She was my poor sister's child as well as Richard's, and my only fear has been that I may love her too deeply, too possessively, and so cramp her freedom.

Perhaps this fear is unfounded. Anyway, it was this that prevented me lifting the telephone receiver then and there on that rainy September night, dialling her number, and asking if all was well. If I had done so, would it have made any difference to what followed? Could I have checked the march of tragedy, then and there, when I woke from that second dream? I didn't know. I still don't know. All I know is that as I sat there in the silent room, listening to the rain beating against my windows out of the night, my fears somehow became clearer—came to a focus, as it were. I knew now, with absolute certainty, that what I feared had something to do with Linda's forthcoming marriage. Her marriage to John Barlow.

But what could it be? What *could* I be afraid of? He was such a pleasant, ordinary young man, from a respected local family; he had a good job; he loved Linda deeply. Well, he seemed to do so. And yet, as I thought about it, as I remembered the uneasiness I always felt in his presence, it occurred to me that this uneasiness—this anxiety for Linda's safety—was always at its height when he made some gesture of affection towards her—a light caress, perhaps—a quick, intimate glance across a crowded room . . .

Common sense. Common sense has been my ally throughout life, and I called in its aid now.

"There is nothing wrong!" I said aloud into the empty room; "There is nothing wrong with this young man!"

And then I went to bed.

It must have been nearly three weeks later when I had the dream again. I had seen Linda in the interval, and she seemed as well and happy as I have ever known her. The only cloud on her horizon was that for the next fortnight John would be working late, and so they wouldn't be able to spend the evenings painting and carpentering together in the new house.

"But I'll go on by myself, Auntie," she assured me; "I want to start on the woodwork in that front room tonight. Pale green, we thought, to go with the pink . . ." So she chattered on, happily and gaily, seeming to make nonsense of my fears.

"It sounds lovely, dear," I said. "Don't knock yourself up, though, working too hard."

For Linda *does* get tired easily. In spite of the thirty years difference in our age, I can always outpace her on our long rambles over the hills and arrive home fresh and vigorous while she is sometimes quite white with exhaustion.

"No, Auntie, don't worry," she said, standing on tiptoe to kiss me—she is such a little thing—"I won't get tired. I'm so happy, I don't think I'll ever get tired again!"

Reassuring enough, you'd have thought. And yet, somehow, it didn't reassure me. Her very happiness—even the irrelevant fact that John would be working late—seemed somehow to add to the intangible peril I could feel gathering round her.

And three nights later I dreamed the dream again.

This time, she was alone in the little house. I don't know how I knew it with such certainty in the dream, but I did—her aloneness seemed to fill the unfurnished rooms with echoes. *She* seemed nervous, too. She was no longer painting with the absorbed concentration of my previous dreams, but jerkily, uncertainly. She kept starting—turning round—listening; and I, hovering somewhere on the stairs as before, seemed to be listening too. Listening for what? For the fear which I knew was creeping like fog into the little house—or for something more?

"It's a dream!" I tried to cry, with soundless lips. "Don't be afraid, Linda, it's only a dream! I've had it before, I'll wake up soon! It's all right, I'm waking right now, I can hear the banging . . ."

I started awake in my chair, bolt upright, deafened by the now familiar thumping of my heart.

But was it my heart? Could that imperious knocking, which shook the house, be merely my heart? The knocking became interspersed with a frantic ringing of the bell. This was no dream. I staggered to my feet, and somehow got down the passage to the front door, and flung it open. There in the rainy night was Linda, Linda wild and white and dishevelled, flinging herself into my arms.

"Oh, Auntie, Auntie, I thought you were out—asleep—I couldn't make you hear—I rang and rang . . ."

I soothed her as best I could. I took her into the kitchen and made her a cup of the weak thin tea she loves, and heard her story.

And after all it wasn't much of a story. Just that she had gone to the new house as usual after work, and had settled down to painting the front room. For a while, she said, she had worked quite happily; and then suddenly she had heard a sound—a shuffling sound, so faint that she might almost have imagined it.

"And that was all, really, Auntie," she said, looking up at me, shamefaced. "But somehow it frightened me so. I ought to have gone and looked round the house, but I didn't dare. I tried to go on working, but from then on there was such an awful feeling—I can't describe it—as if there was something evil in the house—something close behind me—waiting to get its hands round my throat. Oh, Auntie, I know it sounds silly. It's the kind of thing I used to dream when I was a little girl—do you remember?"

Indeed I did remember. I took her on my lap and soothed her now just as I had done then, when she was a little sobbing girl awake and frightened in the depths of the night.

And then I told her she must go home.

"Auntie!" she protested; "But Auntie, can't I stay here with you for the night? That's why I came. I *must* stay!"

But I was adamant. I can't tell you why, but some instinct warned me that, come what may, she must not stay here tonight. Whatever her fear or danger might be elsewhere, they could never be as great as they would be here, in this house, tonight.

So I made her go home, to her lodgings in the town. I couldn't explain it to her, not even to myself. In vain she protested that the last bus had gone, that her old room here was ready for her. I was immovable. I rang up a taxi, and as it disappeared with her round the corner of the lane, casting a weird radiance behind it, I heaved a sigh of relief, as if a great task had been accomplished; as if I had just dragged her to shore out of a dark and stormy sea.

The next morning I found that my instinct had not been without foundation. There *had* been danger lurking round my house last night. For when I went to get my bicycle to go and help about the Mothers' Outing, I found it in its usual place in the shed, but the tyres and mudguard were all spattered with a kind of thick yellow clay. There is no clay like that between here and the village. Where could it have come from? Who had been riding my bicycle through unfamiliar mud in the rain and wind last night? Who had put it back silently in the shed, and gone as silently away?

As I stood there, bewildered and shaken, the telephone rang indoors. It was Linda, and she sounded tense, distraught.

"Auntie, will you do something for me? Will

you come with me to the house tonight, and stay there while I do the painting and—and sort of keep watch for me? I expect you'll think it's silly but I *know* there was somebody there last night—and I'm frightened. Will you come, Auntie?"

There could be only one answer. I got through my day's work as fast as I could, and by six o'clock I was waiting for Linda on the steps of her office. As we hurried through the darkening streets, Linda was apologetic and anxious.

"I know it's awfully silly, Auntie, but John's still working late, and he doesn't even know if he'll finish in time to come and fetch me. I feel scared there without him. And the upstairs lights won't go on again—John hasn't had time to see the electricity people about it yet—and it's so dark and lonely. Do you think someone really *was* there last night, Auntie?"

I didn't tell her about the mud on my bicycle. There seemed no point in alarming her further. Besides, what was there to tell? There was no reason to suppose it had any connection . . .

"Watch out, Auntie, it's terribly muddy along this bit where the builders have been."

I stared down at the thick yellow clay already clinging heavily to my shoes; and straight in front of us, among a cluster of partially finished red brick houses, stood Linda's future home. It stared at us with its little empty windows out of the October dusk. A light breeze rose, but stirred nothing in that wilderness of mud, raw brickwork and scaffolding. Linda and I hesitated, looked at each other.

"Come on," I said, and a minute later we were in the empty house.

We arranged that she should settle down to her painting in the downstairs front room just as if she was alone, and I was to sit on the stairs, near the top, where I could command a view of both upstairs and down. If anyone should come in, by either front or back door, I should see them before they could reach Linda.

It was very quiet as I sat there in the darkness. The light streamed out of the downstairs room where Linda was working, and I could see her through the open door, with her back to me, just as she had been in my dream. How like poor Angela she was, with her pale hair and her white, fragile neck! She was working steadily now, absorbed, confident; reassured, I suppose, by my presence in the house. As I sat, I could feel the step of the stair behind me pressing a little into my spine—a strangely familiar pressure. My whole pose indeed seemed familiar—every muscle seemed to fall into place, as if by long practice, as I sat there, half leaning against the banisters, staring down into the glare of light.

And then, suddenly, I knew. I knew who it was who had cycled in black hatred through the rainy darkness and the yellow mud. I knew who had waited here, night after night, watching Linda as a cat watches a mouse. I knew what was the horror closing in even now on this poor, fragile child—on this sickly, puny brat who had kept *my* lovely, sturdy children from coming into the world; the sons and daughters *I* could have given Richard, tall and strong—the children he should have had—the children *I* could have borne him.

I was creeping downstairs now, on tiptoe, in my stockinged feet, with a light, almost prancing movement, yet silent as a shadow. I could see my hands, clutching in front of me like a lobster's claws, itching for the feel of her white neck. At the foot of the stairs now . . . At the door of the room, and still she worked on, her back to me, oblivious. I tried to cry out, to warn her. "She's coming, Linda!" I tried to scream; "I can see her hands clawing behind you!" But no sound came from my drawn-back lips, no sound from my swift, light feet.

Then, just as in my dream, there were footsteps through the house, quick and loud; a man's footsteps, hurrying—running—rushing. Rushing to save Linda; to save us both.